D0097234

MINA MISTRY
(SORT OF)
INVESTIGATES

Angie Lake

Illustrated by
Ellie O'Shea

Published by Sweet Cherry Publishing Limited
Unit 36, Vulcan House,
Vulcan Road,
Leicester, LE5 3EF
United Kingdom

First published in the US in 2021
2021 edition

2 4 6 8 10 9 7 5 3 1

ISBN: 978-1-78226-887-1

© Sweet Cherry Publishing

Mina Mistry Investigates: The Case of the Disappearing Pets

Written by Angie Lake

All rights reserved. No part of this publication may be
reproduced or utilised in any form or by any means, electronic
or mechanical, including photocopying, recording, or using
any information storage and retrieval system, without prior
permission in writing from the publisher.

The right of Angie Lake to be identified as the author of this
work has been asserted by her in accordance with the Copyright,
Design and Patents Act 1988.

Cover design by Ellie O'Shea and Amy Booth
Illustrations by Ellie O'Shea

Lexile® code numerical measure L = Lexile® 750L

www.sweetcherrypublishing.com

Printed and bound in the UK
E.C007

THE
CASE OF THE
DiSAPPEARING
PETS

Sweet
Cherry

D0097235

PERSONAL FILE:

Name: Mina Snotbridge a.k.a. Mina Mistry

Occupation: Student at Greenville Elementary

Best Friend: Mr. Panda

Second Best Friend: Holly Loafer

Distinguishing Features: Extreme intelligence and ambition. Destined to become a private investigator

Hobbies: Playing the cello, investigating mysteries, and spying on people

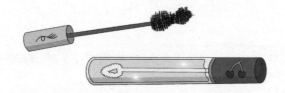

LOG ENTRY #1

Location: My bedroom

Status: General life update

Like every year at school, the first week of October was **SHOWCASE YOUR PETS WEEK**.

I sometimes wonder whether there's

really anything educational about

these themed weeks. I mean, I guess

there was something to learn in

ViKiNG INVASiON RECREATiON WeeK,

even if a lot of it did involve pretending

to beat each other up with homemade

weapons. But I don't know if anyone really

benefited from Historical Moments in

Snooker Week. Sometimes I think that the

teachers just get together, write down a

load of **RANDOM** words on pieces

of paper, and draw a few out of a hat.

Then they just make up an event with

whatever comes out.

I can just imagine it now.

This week, for Showcase Your Pets Week,

the school is full of things about pets. No

one is allowed to bring any **ACTUAL**

PeTS though. Last year somebody

was bitten by a llama. After that, the school

realized that, apart from having animals

in the school being a health and safety

issue—due to some pets going to the toilet

everywhere—it turns out that they don't

have any insurance to cover pet attacks.

For me, **SHOWCASE YOUR PETS WEEK** is even more

complicated than Weird Snooker Thingy

Week. **I DON'T HAVE ANY PETS**. Last year I did a

presentation on Granny Meera's poodle,

Molly. It was about how she limps and hides

behind the sofa whenever she hears a car in the driveway. She's done that ever since my dad accidentally reversed his car into her. I don't think the teachers were impressed. Mrs. Bergenstein said that our project, How to

MOLLY

DAD'S CAR

MOLL

Care for Your Pet, was supposed to be about how and what to feed them, how you groom them, how often you take them for walks …

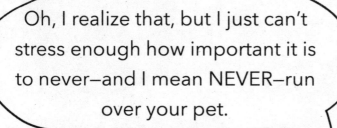

I really wanted a more detailed day-by-day explanation of how to take care of Molly.

Oh, I realize that, but I just can't stress enough how important it is to never—and I mean NEVER—run over your pet.

PERSONAL FILE:

Name: Mrs. Bergenstein

Occupation: Teacher at Greenville

Elementary

Distinguishing Features:

She has a warty ear

Hobbies: She sits

in her car before

school, playing

games on her phone

Somehow, I still scraped by last year, but I knew I'd have to make a bit more effort this year. I still didn't have a pet, so I decided to do a presentation on Mr. Panda. Mr. Panda is my friend and accomplice. My grandad got him for me when I was just a baby and now he helps me **INVESTIGATE** my cases. I knew Mr. Panda wouldn't like me writing about him as if he were a pet, so I have been keeping the project a **SECRET** from him.

Anyway, this morning was the first day of **SHOWCASE YOUR PETS WEEK**. The day everyone in our year had to do their presentations in the assembly hall. This was **NOT** going to be fun …

Holly caught up with me at the school gates. "Morning!" she said cheerfully. "Have you got your presentation ready? Wait till you see mine. Harriet and I have been working on it for **DAYS**."

I don't know how Holly manages to be so bright and cheerful in the mornings. I was still thinking about how COZY it was in bed.

"Yes, it's ready—" I stopped as my brain finished processing what Holly had said. "Hang on … You've been working on your project *with* Harriet?"

"Yes," Holly replied.

"Harriet … your **HAMSTER?**"

"Yes, Harriet my hamster," Holly said, looking at me as if it were really obvious.

Holly carried on talking, but I

didn't pay attention. I couldn't stop

thinking about what she'd just said. It

seemed like there were two possible

scenarios. Either Harriet was, in fact,

A GENiUS HAMSTER

who could talk, write, and had mastered

the art of computer slideshows, and the

presentation was going to be outstanding.

Or Holly had been using Harriet in

some cruel and evil way ... does Holly

have a hamster-wheel-powered desk lamp? **I WOULDN'T BE SURPRISED**...

I shook my head and started listening again. Holly was still talking: "...

Anyway, Mom told me that I can't keep

EXPLOITING Harriet and

that I should give her a rest from all this

homework. She says that it's too much

RESPONSIBILITY for a

hamster and that if I keep overworking

her, she's going to have to get her

animal rights friends to come and talk

to me. I don't see what all the fuss

is about, though. I mean, Harriet is

FABULOUS."

　　We arrived in the assembly hall

and found somewhere to sit. I had a

feeling from Holly's enthusiasm that

her presentation was going to be a lot

better than mine, which is quite worrying

considering that half of it had been done

by a **HAMSTER**.

Mr. Norton, the headmaster, stood on the stage and cleared his throat.

"Good afternoon," he began. "Your teachers have asked you all to prepare a presentation on: **MY PeT'S FAVORiTe THiNG**. I'm sure you've all worked very hard." Mr. Norton looked at us apologetically. "Now, there are a lot of you here and we won't have time to see everybody's presentations, so we've pulled names out of a hat. I'm afraid this means only the students named will do their presentation on stage."

He was interrupted by a hushed cheer from the students. I guess I wasn't the only one not looking forward to doing a presentation in front of the **WHOLE SCHOOL**.

Mr. Norton continued, "After that we have a special guest speaker coming in to give a talk called 'Pets Are People Too'. I hope you'll give a warm welcome to …"

There was a pause as Mr. Norton shuffled through his notes and found the name, "... Professor Lucille Loafer."

Holly **CRiNGeD**. A cry of "Mom! You're so **eMBARRASSiNG!**" escaped her lips. Everyone around her burst into giggles.

Mr. Norton frowned at us.

"So, for our first presentation, can we have ... Mina Snotbridge?"

Great. Just great. I walked toward

the stage and prepared myself to see

how long I could possibly stretch out my

presentation: Mr. Panda's Favorite

Thing and Why I Don't Let Him Do It: Bungee Jumping.

I have to say that my presentation went quite well. Or, to put it another way, it **WASN'T THE WORST**. Danny Dingle had either ignored or forgotten about the pet ban and brought his pet toad in a shoebox, so he failed **INSTANTLY**. This was pretty bad news for Herbie Fisher, called next, who'd had exactly the same idea: he'd brought a shoebox **FULL OF HiS PeT SNAiLS**.

Percy McDuff was almost not allowed to

do his presentation. When he got onstage

with yet another shoebox, Mr. Norton

looked at him very seriously and said,

"Percy, that had better not be a pet in there."

To which Percy answered, "Oh it is, but

don't worry—it's not alive!"

Fortunately, Percy had not

brought the carcass of a **DEAD**,

DECOMPOSiNG animal to

the presentation. He had brought his

homemade pet,

Mr. Shoesie. It

turns out that Mr.

Shoesie is an **OLD SHOe** with a

face painted on it. Apparently, he lives in

the shoebox and doesn't need food or

water, but he does like a lot of exercise.

Ask anyone in school and they'll

probably say that Percy is one sandwich

short of a picnic, but I think it's an act.

I wish I'd thought of painting a face on

something and making up a story about it. And after letting everyone believe the worst, Percy was bound to get a good grade for not bringing in an actual dead animal after all. **GENIUS**.

As suspected, Holly's presentation was actually really good.

It was called **Harriet the Glamour Hamster Loves Posing for Photos.** Holly had taken dozens of photos of Harriet, in **CUTE LITTLE**

OUTFiTS and put them against

different backgrounds. There were

captions like 'Harriet in a gold bikini on a

Malibu beach', 'Harriet in a pink tracksuit

training on her hamster wheel', and

'Harriet in a summer dress having a picnic'.

From the crowd's reaction, this was

clearly everyone's **FAVORiTe**

presentation. Holly had aced it. It was also

a lot less depressing than Millie Mitchel's

presentation: Mr. Bunnykins From

Birth to Death: A Young Rabbit's Struggle with Myxomatosis.

When she'd finished, Mr. Norton had a comment for Millie.

"That was a very touching presentation," he said, "but the theme was supposed to be **MY PET'S FAVORITE THING**, and I don't think your presentation addresses that."

Millie leaned toward the microphone and looked straight at Mr. Norton.

"Sorry. Mr. Bunnykins' favorite thing was not being dead."

There was a muffled round of applause and Millie got down from the stage.

Holly was still **BEAMING TRIUMPHANTLY** from having delivered the best presentation, but her victory was short lived. After a quick break, we all had to return to the assembly hall for Professor Lucille Loafer to give her talk.

Holly cringed as the presentation title flashed up behind her mom: Pets Are People Too: The Cruelty Behind the Making of the Harriet the Hamster Presentation.

Holly looked over at me and mouthed the words, "She's so EMBARRASSING!"

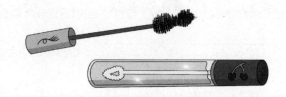

LOG ENTRY #2

Location: Holly's house
Status: General life update

After school, I went over to Holly's house

so we could both work on our projects.

Apparently, after Holly's mom's talk, not

everyone was convinced that Harriet

the Hamster **REALLY** did enjoy

dressing up and having her photo taken.

That meant that it didn't count as her

favorite thing. As Mr. Norton pointed

out, it was more like **HOLLY'S**

FAVORITE THING TO

DO with Harriet, so she'd been asked to

redo her presentation.

Unfortunately, I had to redo

my presentation as well. Nobody

believed that a panda would be into

EXTREME SPORTS like bungee jumping. I wanted to explain that Mr. Panda was **no ordinary panda** and that he was using stereotypical panda behavior to disguise his **TRUE IDENTITY**, but I didn't want to blow his cover. The result of all this was that Holly and I were crawling around the garden, hunting for **NEW PETS**.

Well, when I say that Holly and I

were crawling around the garden, it

was more a case of **me crawling**

around the garden and Holly saying

HELPFUL THINGS like:

"Dig a little there, on the right," or "Try to get right underneath that bush."

Apparently Holly couldn't do any of the **actual crawling** around in the **DiRT** because, despite usually having an outfit for **eveRY** occasion, she didn't have an outfit for this one.

We hoped that we'd find something like a hedgehog, a field mouse, or even a frog that we could adopt. We thought we could look after something for a week, then put it back in the garden. We had to give up on that idea when it got dark, though. I picked up the cookie tin containing the pets I'd found so far, and we headed back into the house.

We sat at the kitchen table.

"Okay," said Holly brightly, **"LET'S HAVE iT ... WHAT HAVE WE FOUND?"**

I grabbed a **PENCIL** and had a bit

of a poke around in the leaves and mud.

"Okay ... we have one **SLUG** and ...

one **EARTHWORM**."

"**UGH!** Gross!" Holly wrinkled her

nose. "Okay, I suppose we'll have to work

with what we've got." She sighed and opened up her laptop.

"Right …" she said after a moment of typing. "According to this, earthworms eat decomposing organic matter found in the **SOiL**, like leaves and bits of fruit." Holly's eyes swept over the search page. "Oh, good! Slugs eat the same thing! Okay, so we can just put them in a container with a load of dirt from the garden, you can keep them

in **YOUR ROOM** for a few days,

and then we can let them go."

"Okay, cool!" I replied.

Then, a realization

struck me. I

narrowed my

eyes.

"**HANG
ON A
MINUTE**...

why do I have to keep them in *my* room?

Why can't we keep them in *your* room?"

Holly put her hands on her hips.

"You can't be serious! Mina, one day

I'll be **FAMOUS**.

If the story gets out

that I once had a

pet slug and a pet

earthworm it could

ruin my career as a

CELEBRITY."

45

Holly and I were still arguing about who was going to get stuck with the slug and the earthworm when we heard a key in the door. We could hear Holly's mom **TALKiNG LOUDLY** on her mobile phone as she walked through the house toward the kitchen.

"… Great, okay … and did you get them all? Every last one? … Excellent! … We'll show them at the protest! … Okay, I'm home, I have to go, talk tomorrow!"

Holly's mom swung open the kitchen door and looked surprised to see us. "Girls! Hi! I wasn't expecting you to be here."

"We were just about to go upstairs to get on with our **PROJECT**," said Holly, glaring. "You know, the project I'd already finished but now I have to start again thanks to you?"

"Hello darling, nice to see you too," said Holly's mom. She leaned over to give Holly a quick kiss on the top of the head on her way to the coffee machine.

Holly fumed silently.

"Now darling," Holly's mom continued, "I'm just trying to teach you to take better care of Harriet. She's a hamster: she needs fresh wood shavings, food and water ... not **DiAMANTe TiARAS** and her own **SOCiAL MeDiA HANDLeS**." She was really getting into it now. "When I ask you if you've changed Harriet, I mean have you cleaned

out her cage and put in fresh bedding?

Not have you remembered to put her

in casual sportswear. I mean, the way

137 POSTS 291 FOLLOWERS 1 FOLLOWING

HARRIET.HAMSTER

you mess around with that hamster, it's **AWFUL**. You treat her like she's some sort of—of …"

"Guinea pig?" I supplied helpfully.

Holly's mom looked grim. "I'm being serious. I think you both need to take **ANIMAL WELFARE** more seriously. Why don't you come with me to the big protest this weekend? Face Gunk have just opened a makeup factory on the outskirts of town and—"

Holly's ears suddenly pricked up and she spun around to face her mom. "Face Gunk? Did you say *Face Gunk* have opened a factory here, in this town?"

"Well yes," replied Holly's mom. "And it's **AWFUL!** You know what these big makeup companies are like; they probably test all their products on animals. I mean, do you know what they do to those poor creatures? They take those sweet, defenseless little mice and rabbits and they cover them in lipstick and eye shadow! **HOW WOULD YOU LIKE THAT?**"

Holly was completely lost in a fantasy world of cherry-flavored lip gloss and sparkly eye shadow.

"Face Gunk," Holly breathed reverently. "Right here in our town! Did you know that they sponsor *Just 17*? I wonder if I could meet them ..."

I butted in to reply to Holly's mom. "I wouldn't like it, just for the record."

Suddenly something in Holly's head clicked and her mom's words finally registered.

"So **HANG ON** ..." she said. "You're telling me that there are animals whose job is to just sit around all day trying out makeup? **WOW**, just wait until I tell Harriet!"

I gave her a look. "I think you're missing the point, Holly. **IT'S NOT A GOOD THiNG.**"

"Thank you, Mina!" said Holly's mom, nodding. "Anyway, I'm going to speak to a few friends from the animal rights group. I'll let you girls know about the date and time of the protest. Now, run along and get going with your project.

Oh! And Holly, can you please make sure

HARRIET HAS FOOD AND WATER?"

We made our way upstairs with our

tin of pets. Holly was in a world of her

own, mumbling things like, "I wonder if Face Gunk will be offering discounts to local celebrities?" and "Maybe I could be the **NEW FACE** of Face Gunk … their new Gunk Girl …"

Meanwhile, I was trying to come up with names for our new pets. I quite liked **SLUGLY BUGLY** for the slug—it made him sound a lot cuter than he really was. I was a bit stuck on a good name for an earthworm though. I was having trouble choosing between Sammy and Barnacle.

Suddenly Holly cried out. **"MINA, QUICK! HELP!"**

Holly was standing by Harriet's cage. She turned me. "Can you see Harriet anywhere? She's not in her cage!"

Holly and I turned her room upside-down and inside-out but Harriet the hamster was **NOWHERE** to be found.

Holly sat on her bed and **BURST** into tears.

I sat next to her and put an arm around her shoulders. "Holly, don't cry! **WE'LL FIND HER.** Listen, let's make some posters and put them up around the neighborhood. Someone must have seen her."

Holly nodded as she wiped her snot and tears away with a tissue.

"Now," I said. "I'm just going to take a **few notes** so we can get her description and put out an **APB**."

Holly looked at me wide-eyed. "What's an APB?"

"Oh, I've heard them use the term on police shows," I said airily. "I think it means 'Absent Pet Bulletin'."

"Oh, okay. Good," said Holly uncertainly. Then she said, "Er … Mina … did you just make that up?"

I nodded. "Yes—yes I did. Now, we have to find a **RECENT PHOTO** of Harriet."

Holly managed a little smile. "I have hundreds, take your pick."

"Okay!" I smiled back. "And I need you to try to remember, what was she wearing the last time you saw her?"

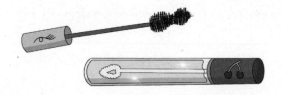

LOG ENTRY #3

Location: My bedroom

Status: Reporting on the scene of a crime

Holly was still quite upset when I left her

and started making my way home on

my scooter. She was being **VERY**

DRAMATIC and had even changed into a black mourning outfit, with a matching black hat, black veil, and black handkerchief. What normal person has an outfit to wear to funerals, but doesn't have a single item of clothing suitable for crawling around in the mud? I sometimes think that Holly is missing out on life.

Anyway, I was making my way home through the town with Slugly Bugly and Sammy the Earthworm tucked

away safely in a tin in my backpack. My

folder was **FULL** of flyers that we

had printed out at Holly's house. It had been quite a hard task. I'd never seen Holly take a project so seriously before. We spent hours going through photos of Harriet because Holly insisted on finding a picture that showed her 'best angle', *and* we had to make sure that she wasn't wearing anything from last season. As Holly told me, "Harriet is a **FABULOUS** hamster and she deserves a **FABULOUS** flyer."

MISSING
HARRIET THE HAMSTER
STRAWBERRY BLONDE FUR, EYES LIKE
DARK CHOCOLATE.

Last seen on Windsor Terrace on Sunday the 16th wearing a beige velvet jumpsuit with gold trim.

 Please email Holly with any information at:
hollyglam@yoohoo.com

I started putting our flyers up on my way home. I was in the middle of taping one to the window of Greenville Groceries when I came face-to-face with Percy and a **VERY** upset-looking Danny. They were putting up flyers too.

I called over to them. "Hey! What's wrong?"

Danny didn't answer.

He looked like he was about to burst into

tears. Percy silently handed me a flyer.

MISSING

Most awesome genius toad EVER

Please return immediately to Danny Dingle

Thank you

I knew how much Danny's toad

meant to him. "Oh my goodness!

SUPERDOG'S GONE

MISSING?!"

Danny just turned away.

"He's nowhere to be found," said Percy.

"We've looked everywhere: our clubhouse,

Danny's garden … everywhere."

I was a bit worried about Percy's

definition of 'everywhere'. I guess

this showed that Percy and Danny

probably don't get out much. Maybe the clubhouse and the garden really was **EVERYWHERE** to them.

Suddenly, I made a connection. I narrowed my eyes. "I don't know if this is just a coincidence, **BUT LOOK** ..."

I handed Percy one of my flyers.

"Harriet the hamster has gone missing too?"

Danny spun around to look at the flyer. It seemed he had put two and two together and actually come up with four for once.

"Wait a minute," he said, staring at the flyer. "Do you think there's a **CONNECTION?** Do you think that maybe Harriet and Superdog met, fell in love, and **RAN AWAY TOGETHER?**"

I didn't know what to say to that.

"I'm not going to rule out any

possibilities," I answered diplomatically.

"Have you put up a lot of flyers yet?"

I asked, trying to steer the conversation

away from any more **WEiRD**

SPECULATION about

toads and hamsters running off

together.

Danny and Percy

looked back along the

high street. I followed

their gaze. Every single lamp post, bin, bush, bench and ... well, absolutely **EVERYTHING** had a Superdog flyer taped to it.

"Ah ..." this was awkward. "It's just that you haven't put a phone number on it. Or an email address."

Danny and Percy both managed to look even more deflated. "Oh," they sighed.

We were suddenly distracted by the sound of **SIRENS**. They seemed to be heading to the end of the high

street. We instantly started running in that

direction, like good, helpful, nosy citizens.

   We stopped outside the pet shop

where a small crowd had gathered.

The entrance was blocked off with

yellow tape that read: **POLICE**

LINE, DO NOT CROSS.

PC McApple was standing by the

doorway taking the owner's statement.

I discretely made my way through the

crowd to get **AS CLOSE AS POSSIBLE** and see what I could find out.

I got to the doorway just in time to hear PC McApple ask, "So when did you discover the break in?"

"About half an hour ago," replied the pet shop owner, worriedly. "Our shop doesn't open on Mondays, but I still have to come in and feed the animals. I let myself in and then discovered this **HUGE HOLE** in the floor. There was rubble everywhere … it was almost like there'd been an **EXPLOSION**. I went to check on the animals and all the pens were open— the animals were all missing."

PC McApple wrote all of this down. "Do you have any idea who might have done this?"

"Well, I do have one clue …" said the pet shop owner. "I found this note under the door last week." she handed PC McApple a

folded piece of paper. The officer unfolded

it and read it out loud:

"STOP ANIMAL CRUELTY.
KEEPING ANIMALS IN CAGES IS WRONG.
RELEASE THE ANIMALS OR PAY THE PRICE."

I frowned. Something about that note seemed familiar.

PC McApple looked confused. "Do you have any idea who this could be from?"

The pet shop owner looked back at him blankly. "No, I was rather hoping you could help me out with that."

"Hmm …" said PC McApple. "Yes … Er … We'll keep hold of this note as evidence. I'll pass it on to the forensics team, see what they can find out." PC McApple dropped the note into a Ziplock bag and closed his notebook.

I slipped away quietly through the crowd and walked back to where Danny and Percy were standing. They both looked at me expectantly.

"So ... what did you find out?" asked Danny.

"It sounds serious," I said. "All of the pets have been taken. It looks like there's not a **SiNGLe PeT** in Greenville that's safe. I'm not too sure that PC McApple can handle this on his own."

We all looked over at PC McApple. He was walking around, intently looking for something.

"What's he doing now?" asked Danny.

"He's looking for his pencil," I replied.

Percy squinted at him. "The pencil that's behind his ear?" he asked.

I nodded. "Yes, I think so. He was scratching his head with it earlier. He must have forgotten where he left it. I think we'd better arrange an **EMERGENCY MEETING** with all the other kids in town. We need to let everybody know about this."

"Okay," said Danny, "we'll hold it at Percy's house tomorrow, **STRAiGHT AFTeR SCHOOL**."

"Yeah!" Percy nodded enthusiastically. Then his face fell. "Wait … my mom will never allow that. Mom's still **ANGRY** about the time we played rotten fruit wars and used the upstairs window for target practice. Apparently, all that rotten fruit rolled into the gutter, and now she says she can't sleep at night for the sound of

RATS scuttling on the roof. Can't we hold it at Danny's house?"

We both looked at Danny.

He shook his head. "Negative. Mom is still **FUMiNG** from when Dad and I built a miniature golf course in the back garden."

85

I frowned. That didn't sound right.

"Really? But that sounds cool! What's wrong with that?"

"Well," Danny continued, "she didn't like that we pulled up the dining room carpet to use as flooring and cut it into the shape of the golf course. Or that we got bored of the project and left the carpet out in the rain …"

AH. That sounded more like Danny. We did still need somewhere for our meeting though. "I don't know if my mom and dad would let me hold a meeting …" I said, dubiously.

"Okay, we'll have to do it at Holly's house," said Danny. "I'm sure she'll understand: this is a **LOCAL EMERGENCY** and we have to intervene. Mina, get the word out to as many kids as possible. Percy and I will do the same. Good luck, and see you tomorrow!"

At that, we all went our separate ways. I had a lot of information in my head and

I needed to get home and discuss it with Mr. Panda. **There were a few things that didn't add up.**

In the past 24 hours there had been at least **THREE** separate cases of animal disappearances ... **COINCIDENCE?** I didn't think so. According to the pet shop owner, the thieves had blown a hole underneath the shop and let themselves in through the floor. But how did they get under the building in the first place? How did they get away afterward? Did they have a getaway car? And, more to the point, how did they **escape**, completely unnoticed, with all those animals?

What did they want the animals for anyway?

When I got home, I went straight to the fridge for a snack. There was a note stuck to the fridge door:

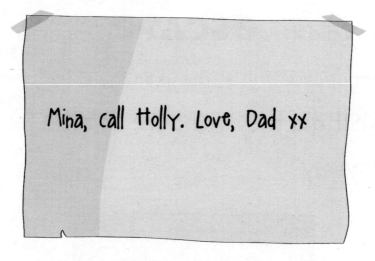

Mina, call Holly. Love, Dad xx

I had been going to call her anyway: I needed to tell her about the emergency meeting. I grabbed a yogurt and a spoon,

then I went in search of the phone so I

could call Holly from my room.

"Holly, what's happening? Do you have any news about Harriet?"

"No. I was going to ask you the same thing."

It was time to bring up the subject of the **EMERGENCY MEETING**. I had to think of a way of getting Holly on board with the idea of having the meeting at her house, seeing as it's quite rude to organize this sort of thing without asking first …

"Sorry Holly," I said. "No news about Harriet yet, but I do have something important to tell you. The pet shop in town has been **BROKEN INTO!**

All the pets have been stolen and Danny's pet toad has gone missing too. Danny, Percy and I agreed that we should have an emergency meeting tomorrow after school. Would you like to hold it at your house? Just because, you know, seeing as you're the local celebrity and you've been affected too, I thought you might want to show solidarity with the people of Greenville … It's very important—it looks like all the pets in

Greenville might be in **DANGER**."

Holly went quiet for a bit, as if she were trying to work out what everyone else's pets going missing had to do with her and whether it was something she should care about. I thought I'd better pull out all the stops to make the idea more interesting to her. "I mean, I've been turning it over and I thought that maybe you could even be our **SPOKESPERSON!** In case the newspapers want to interview us?"

This caught Holly's attention. "Don't worry," she replied. "We can have the meeting at my house. I'll spread the word." There was a slight pause followed by a gasp. "Hang on a minute, did you say it's tomorrow? I'd better go! I need to find something to wear to the meeting."

And at that, Holly hung up.

It was time for me to get to work. I popped my head out my bedroom door to double check that there was no one home. Then I went into the back of my wardrobe and found a box marked: Old Toys. From it, I took out **MY SECRET LOG** and a new case file. Then I turned to look for Mr. Panda.

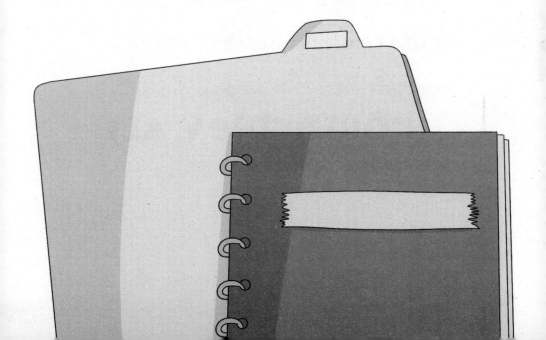

He was sitting on my bed reading a paragliding magazine. I didn't like to interrupt him, but I did need his help.

We discussed it. As things stood, we had one crime: the pet shop burglary. Then there were two cases of missing pets. **COULD THEY ALL BE RELATED?**

The only significant evidence so far

was an anonymous note found at the pet

shop. It read:

'STOP ANIMAL CRUELTY.
KEEPING ANIMALS IN CAGES IS WRONG.
RELEASE THE ANIMALS OR PAY THE PRICE.'

It sounded like something that Holly's

mom or one of her friends from the

ANiMAL WeLFARe GROUP would write if they were really angry.

I thought about motives. Releasing the animals for humane reasons was one possible explanation. And, of course, there was always the possibility that someone **STOLe THe ANiMALS TO SeLL THeM**.

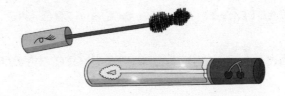

LOG ENTRY #4

Location: My bedroom

Status: Reporting on the emergency meeting

The meeting at Holly's house didn't go

EXACTLY as planned, mainly

because the only people who came were

Danny and Percy (who organized the meeting), Holly (who lives there anyway), Gareth Trumpshaw (the only person that Holly thought to invite), Herbie Fisher (the kid with the snail farm who heard about the meeting from Gareth), and me … so much for Holly's promise to 'spread the word'.

Herbie Fisher's **SNAiL FARM** had disappeared between Monday afternoon and Tuesday morning, so we had another **PeT DiSAPPeARANCe** on our hands. Although, for the life of me I couldn't imagine why anybody would want to steal a box of snails. I mean, if anything a box of snails is something you'd leave under someone's bed or in their lunchbox as a joke.

We all sat around the kitchen table whilst Holly acted like the perfect hostess and served us all juice and tiny triangular sandwiches. She was really turning on the charm for Gareth.

I had to admit, it was a pretty good idea of Danny's to arrange the meeting at Holly's house. It was by far the nicest place, though it seemed colder than usual today, which was odd. Still, I would never have thought to serve food and drinks, and last time we had a meeting in Danny's clubhouse the jelly Danny's dad gave us made us **FART** so much that we ended up being sick out of the windows.

You wouldn't catch Holly farting or being sick out of a window. For starters, she'd rather die than fart in front of Gareth and, **MORE IMPORTANTLY**, she doesn't have an outfit for that sort of activity.

We were just going over the facts when Holly's mom, who'd come into the kitchen to get a cappuccino, interrupted, "Don't you all think it's a bit of a coincidence that all the animals in town have started to go missing

since Face Gunk opened their **NEW**

MAKEUP FACTORY?"

We all looked up at her.

"What do you mean, Mom?" said Holly.

Holly's mom put her cup down on

the table. "Well … we all know that most

of these factories test their products

on animals. Those poor little creatures

are probably locked up in a lab, being smeared with **LiP GLOSS** and **MASCARA**."

Holly rolled her eyes. "Really, Mom? I happen to know that **FACE GUNK** don't test makeup on animals! Look it up if you don't believe me. And even if they did, I'm pretty sure they wouldn't go around breaking into pet shops or **STEALING PEOPLE'S PETS**."

The look on Holly's face told me that

she'd been hit by another thought. She

turned dramatically to face her mother.

"On the other hand … this does

sounds very much like something your

ANiMAL RiGHTS activist

friends might do: creep around when

nobody is looking and release any

animals they find in cages."

Holly did have a point.

"Don't be ridiculous Holly." Holly's

mom picked up her coffee and chuckled

uneasily. "My friends and I protest

peacefully. We would never *steal* animals.

I don't know where you get your ideas

from." She walked out of the kitchen

sipping her coffee.

WE ALL LOOKED AT EACH OTHER. Gareth

was the first to speak. "So we have two

suspects: The makeup factory and Holly's

mom and her friends."

"Hang on a minute!" said Holly. "I'm pretty sure this has **NOTHiNG** to do with the makeup factory."

I frowned. "How can you be so sure?"

"Because I just am, okay?" Holly gave us all a very stern look. Then she looked at the clock on the microwave and jumped up. "Oh! I'm going to be late. You'd all better get going."

Percy had been stuffing sandwiches into his mouth all meeting. He quickly grabbed another three, sensing that

teatime was nearly over.

Danny looked forlorn. "But the meeting

... The **PeTS** ..."

"Sorry guys," said Holly. "We'll have

to continue another time; there's

somewhere I need to be."

And that was that. One

minute Holly was feeding

us little sandwiches, the

next she was throwing

us out onto the street. But that's Holly for you: **ALL EXTREMES**.

It was probably for the best that we all had to leave when we did, I was starting to feel like there were too many people involved in the investigation. I'd much rather work on my own; it's a lot safer.

I hurried home. I had a lot to tell Mr. Panda:

I wanted to run the Face Gunk theory by him and see what he thought. It didn't sound like Holly had actually researched it. I suspected that she just didn't want anyone offending the makers of her favorite fruity-flavored lip balms. It looked like we may have **ANOTHER SUSPECT** after all.

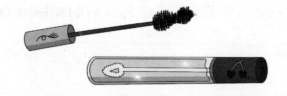

LOG ENTRY #5

Location: My bedroom
Status: Conducting serious detective work

I went straight to the fridge when I got home, but there were no messages. This was usually good news, as it meant that

Dad hadn't been asked to work late on

a secret mission, and he'd be home for

dinner for once.

I went to the cookie jar

and found half a packet

of ginger nut cookies.

That should make Mr. Panda

happy—he loves ginger

nut cookies.

Then I went up to my room to pick

up Mr. Panda and the case file, before

heading to the attic. I wanted to have a look at Dad's model train set. Don't worry, I wasn't interested in the actual trains. I wanted to have a look at the model town to see if there was anything I might have missed. As I've mentioned before, Dad's model train set runs around a precisely scaled model of Greenville. He spends hours in the attic **SPYiNG** on the neighbors to see if anyone has made any changes to their houses, like putting up a satellite dish, painting a fence, or adding a swimming pool. (It turns out that not many people add swimming pools, so Dad's stuck with a whole box of model swimming pools he's just waiting to use.)

Whilst I was looking at the model town, I told Mr. Panda about our **TWO KEY THEORIES**:

1. Animal rights campaigners released the animals in way of protest.

or

2. Face Gunk took the animals to use them for animal testing.

Mr. Panda was horrified that anyone would do something like that to cute little animals. I promised him I'd get to the bottom of it.

I located Holly's house, the pet shop, and Danny's house in Dad's model town.

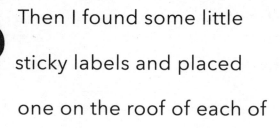

Then I found some little sticky labels and placed one on the roof of each of

these places. After a little more thinking, I found the Face Gunk factory on the outskirts of town and stuck labels on that too.

I took a step back to see if any patterns emerged.

... NOTHiNG.

Then I remembered that Herbie Fisher's snails had gone missing, so I put a label on his house too and took a step back again.

... STiLL NOTHiNG.

I felt a bit disappointed. I was hoping I would find *something*. The only thing I'd worked out is that I seemed to be coming down with a cold.

I looked at Mr. Panda and said, "Well, I guess the next step in the **iNVESTiGATiON** is going to be to infiltrate Face Gunk, which is right next to the **SEWAGE TREATMENT PLANT**." I rolled my eyes and added, "Nice place for it!"

Mr. Panda and I finished our cookies

before heading back downstairs to my room.

The next day I took my scooter to

school so I could go straight to Face

Gunk at the end of the day. I was

definitely coming down with a cold. My

nose was bunged up and I had spent

all morning **SNEEZiNG** and

SPLUTTERING, much to Holly's disgust.

It was a long scoot to Face Gunk. It's on the outskirts of town and not in an area I usually visit. When I arrived, I left my scooter hidden in some bushes outside a place called Hope Farm and waited for my opportunity.

It was a delicate operation, but I managed to **SNEAK** through the security control at the front gate by hiding behind a delivery van. I knew that I'd never get in through the main entrance, so I walked around the building and found a side door. I hid behind a nearby bush and waited.

After what felt like **FOREVER**, I finally saw the door open. An employee walked out, tapping furiously

on their phone, and left the door open.

I saw my chance to make a run for it.

Just as I made it through the door, I
SNeeZeD. The door hadn't
fully closed, and I was petrified that
the worker I had just seen would come
back inside and catch me. I held my
hands over my nose and mouth to stop
myself sneezing again and **FROZe**.
I stayed like that until I felt I was out of
danger. Then I put my hand down and

looked around: **FINALLY, I WAS INSIDE!**

 RECEPTIO

 WAITING

MARKET

TESTING

DIRECTO

INFORM

I had no idea where I was supposed to be going, so I wandered around the hallways for a bit. **BINGO!** I came across an emergency escape plan. It showed me where all the exits were, where the factory floor was, and—**EUREKA!**—where the laboratory was.

I planned my route. It looked like there was nothing I could hide behind along any of the corridors. So I decided to make a run for it. I took a deep breath

and dashed down the hallway, turned left at the end of it, and headed for the first door on the right. It had a sign on, which read: **TESTING AREA— DO NOT ENTER**.

I'd found it!

I began to gently push the door open, but someone on the other side must have been pulling it open at the same time. I **TRIPPED OVER** my feet as I flew into the room. A rather surprised-looking lady in a lab coat stared down at me. She helped me up to my feet.

The lady frowned worriedly. "Okay, so, two things. First, are you alright?"

I dusted myself off as I got to my feet.
"Yes, I'm fine, thanks."

She nodded. "Right. Second, what are you doing here?"

I hadn't thought this far ahead so I just said the very first thing that came to mind.

"I'm looking for my friend."

It wasn't the **MOST CONVINCING** argument, so it was very lucky when Holly appeared as if from nowhere.

"Oh, Holly," I said, as

ENTHUSIASTICALLY

as I could. "There you are! I've been

looking for you everywhere."

133

Holly looked at me suspiciously. "Right ..."

The lady in the lab coat looked down at

Holly. "Is this girl with you?"

Holly switched on her

100-KiLOWATT SMiLe.

"Mina? Yes, well I asked her to

stop by here to pick me up."

She turned to me. "You didn't have to come all the way inside, Mina! You could have waited for me outside, you know!"

Holly grabbed me by the arm and pulled me cheerfully but firmly along the hallway, past the reception, and out through the front door.

None of this made any sense!

"What's happening Holly? **WHAT ARE YOU DOING HERE?**"

"Shh! Keep moving, we'll talk later,"

Holly replied.

Holly directed me off the factory

grounds and toward the bushes outside

Hope Farm.

Holly was the first to speak. "Mina, what on earth were you doing in there? You could have got into **LOADS OF TROUBLE!**"

"I was investigating the testing area to see if the **MISSING PETS** were there!" I replied. "But what were you doing there?"

Holly looked a bit panicky. "Oh ... err ... me too! I was investigating the testing ... thing ..." She trailed off awkwardly.

I wasn't sure that Holly was telling the whole truth.

I raised an eyebrow, "And how did you get in, exactly?"

Holly sighed. "Look, we have to keep this a secret, but I know someone who works there. I can't tell you everything, but they **DEFINITELY** don't test their products on animals and there were no pets to be found anywhere."

My mind was reeling. Holly was

investigating this too? "But how come—"

Holly interrupted me. "I can't answer any more questions about this, Mina. You're just going to have to trust me.

FACE GUNK HAS NOTHING TO DO WITH THE MISSING PETS."

I was itching to know how Holly had managed to infiltrate Face Gunk before me. After all, I'm supposed to be the **PRIVATE**

iNVeSTiGATOR here. All I

knew was that she must really be missing

Harriet the Hamster to go to these lengths.

I found my scooter hidden in the

bushes just where I'd left it. Then Holly

and I walked back toward the town.

"What are you going to do now?" I

asked.

"I'm going to pick up some little

earrings I ordered for Harriet from the

jewelry shop in town!" said Holly.

"I'll give them to her when—" her face fell,

"… *if* I ever see her again. Want to come

with me?"

I didn't feel like staying out. I was still

feeling quite ill, but Holly did seem a bit

sad. In any case, the jewelry shop was next to the **PET SHOP**, and they were both on my way home.

"I'll walk there with you," I decided, "but after that I should probably go home. I have a terrible cold."

I scooted home as **FAST** as I could after parting with Holly outside the shop. I felt like one giant swollen head, filled to the brim with headache and snot, but I was glad that at least we'd managed to **SCRATCH ONE SUSPECT FROM OUR LIST**.

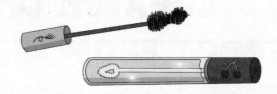

LOG ENTRY #6

Location: My bedroom

Status: Feeling a bit sorry for myself

As soon as I got home, I got into bed.

Mr. Panda and I talked about **THE CASE**. It might have been because I was feeling a bit hazy and full of cold, but

lots of things didn't really seem to add up.

There was **NO TRACE** of any

of the animals anywhere, and on top of

that, Holly was acting weird. How could she

even afford to buy Harriet the

hamster new

earrings? She'd just spent all her birthday
money buying herself and Harriet matching
ski suits.

I also wasn't too sure about the

THEORY that Holly's mom and

her animal welfare friends had released

all the animals either. I mean, they *could*

have written the note at the pet shop, but

would they have released Harriet and

Superdog too? And the crime that made

the least sense was the disappearance of

Herbie Fisher's snail farm. Why would

anyone want a snail

farm?

UH OH! Thinking about snails suddenly reminded me about the project I'd been working on with Holly. I had moved Slugly Bugly and Sammy the Earthworm into a box, and they'd had some fresh dirt and grime from the garden, but I'd **COMPLETELY FORGOTTEN** about them since then. I was supposed to be checking up on them regularly. I had a sinking feeling that something terrible might have happened to them. Holly was not going to be pleased

if I put our projects in jeopardy.

I opened the box and started poking

around with a pencil to see if they were still

alive. I found Slugly Bugly, but there was

NO SiGN of Sammy the Earthworm.

I inspected the box to see if there were any holes he could have escaped through. **THERE WAS NOTHING**.

Then I had a chilling thought and went online to do some research. There I discovered that some species of predatory slugs actually eat earthworms.

I took another look in the box. Slugly definitely looked a lot fatter. I'd have to think very carefully about how to break the news to Holly. Hopefully she hadn't

already gone out and bought Sammy any clothes or jewelry.

We'd also have to rethink our project. I just wasn't too sure how to frame it. My first thought was: Slugly Bugly's Favorite Thing: Sammy the Earthworm. A short-lived friendship.

I was in bed, curled around my notebook, puzzling it all over when I heard a door open downstairs. Dad was home. I dragged myself

upright as Dad poked his

head around the door.

"Are you alright, dear?

You don't look too well,"

he said.

I shook my head. "No, I think I'm coming down with a cold."

"Would you like me to make you a cup of your granny Meera's famous **CARDAMOM COCOA?**" he asked.

That was exactly what I needed. "Yes, please!"

"Then why don't you go up to the attic?" said Dad. "I'll make us both a cup of cocoa and I'll be right up."

I grabbed a box of tissues from my bedside table and **DRAGGED** myself upstairs to the attic. It was cozy up there. I switched Dad's train set on. The trains started chugging around the model of Greenville as all the houses and streetlights lit up. I found a blanket and curled up in a chair as I watched the miniature village coming to life.

The smell of cardamom cocoa wafted up the stairs and a few seconds later Dad

walked in. He passed me a cup of cocoa and sat next to me, looking at the model trains.

"I see you've marked some of the buildings with stickers. It looks like you're looking for some sort of pattern?"

I didn't say anything. I wasn't about to tell Dad about my investigation.

"Loose lips sink ships," Dad often

156

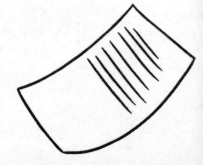

says. When you have a **SECRET INVESTIGATION**, you never know who could be listening in or how. There could be bugs anywhere. It's best to be careful and to give only the minimum information. This had to be a test; we never talk about work.

I leaned over the model town to take another look. Then Dad said, "I'm sure you'll work it out, the answer is probably right under your nose."

At that moment a **LARGE BLOB OF SNOT** dripped from my nose. It landed right onto the little model jewelry shop.

I wiped my face. "**OOPS!** Sorry!"

"Don't worry about it," Dad replied.

I grabbed a bit of tissue to clean everything up. Suddenly, **I NOTICED SOMETHING.**

"Dad ... there's **SOMETHING MISSING** in your model town."

Dad frowned. "Really? Where?"

"Next to the Face Gunk factory," I said. "You have a field but there should be a farmhouse there too."

Dad took a closer look at his model town. "Are you sure?"

I nodded. "Positive. I passed it yesterday. There's a place there called **HOPE FARM**."

"Do you have any idea what they do?" he asked.

"No," I replied. "I was about to ask you the same thing."

"I'd better find out then," said Dad. "Leave it to me."

I still wasn't feeling well the next day, so Dad called the school to tell them I'd be staying at home. I figured I could at least do a bit of work on the Slugly Bugly project seeing as Holly was 'too busy',

although she couldn't tell me what with.

I slept for a bit in the morning, then

I checked on Slugly and did a bit of

work on our project. After that, I went

upstairs to the attic to look at Dad's

model of Greenville again. Suddenly,

I REMEMBERED

SOMETHING that the pet shop

owner had said when she was being

interviewed by PC McApple. She said

that the burglars had got into the shop by **BLOWING A HOLE** in the floor.

I had wondered about it at the time, but now it clicked. There was only one way they could have done that: **THE SEWERS!**

The thieves must have blown their way into the shop from the sewers … and if that's how they got in, that must have been how they got the animals out.

There were probably some clues right underneath **THE PET SHOP!** This was big! This was **URGENT!** There might even be injured pets down there. I realized that I'd have to go and **INVESTIGATE**, but it would have to be under the cover of darkness. I was

going to have to sneak out in the middle of the night and crawl though the sewers.

I really didn't feel like crawling through the sewers on my own in the middle of the night though, so I thought I'd get Danny, Percy, and Holly to come with me. It's their pets that we were looking for, after all.

I didn't doubt for a second that Danny and Percy would jump at the chance of crawling through **GRiMe** and **MUCK**, but there was no way

Holly was going to agree to it. I mean,
I couldn't even get her to kneel down
in her own back garden. I was going
to have to change the story slightly.
Instead of letting on that we were
crawling through the sewers, I'd have
to tell her we'd be taking a shortcut
through an **UNDERGROUND
AQUEDUCT** or something.

Even if she believed that, it was
still going to be tricky to get Holly

to come along. She was definitely

going to complain about not having

a **SUITABLE OUTFIT**.

Maybe I could ask Danny and Percy to

help with that. I'm not very good at this

sort of thing, but Danny and Percy are

very good at making things for this kind of

emergency.

I went back downstairs to my room and I

emailed everyone:

To: Danny Dingle, Percy McDuff, Holly Loafer

Cc:

Subject: Help Me Find Missing Pets

From: Mina Mistry

Hi guys,

I think I know where we can find Harriet and

Superdog (and maybe even Herbie's snails), but I'll need

your help. Call me this afternoon to discuss the details.

Mina

Then I sent Danny and Percy a second email.

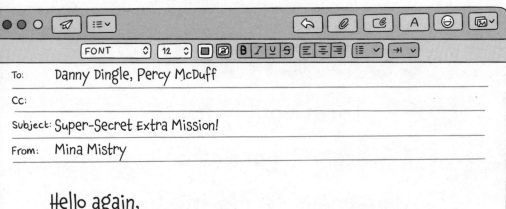

To: Danny Dingle, Percy McDuff

Cc:

Subject: Super-Secret Extra Mission!

From: Mina Mistry

Hello again,

I have an extra mission for you. I need you to make us all outfits we can wear to help us stay clean and dry in a slimy situation. What did you guys wear in that science club rafting challenge again?

Mina

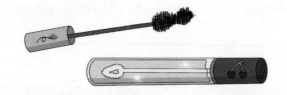

LOG ENTRY #7

Location: My house

Status: Reporting on our

dangerous secret mission

As I expected, Holly was **NOT**

HAPPY. She was not happy about

creeping out of her house at three o'clock

in the morning, she was not happy about

Danny and Percy solving her outfit problem

by wrapping her up in **GARBAGE**

BAGS AND

STiCKY

TAPe, and

she was not

happy about

wandering around

in an 'underground

aqueduct'.

171

It was four in the morning by the time Danny and Percy put the finishing touches to our outfits. Then we found a manhole close to the pet shop that lead down into **THE SEWERS**.

We all climbed down. I went first, then Holly, then Percy, then Danny. The idea had been not to let Holly go last, as she'd begged to. This was because we knew there was a good chance that she'd wait for us all to climb down, then run away.

It probably wasn't the best idea to make her

go before Percy, though. Percy took one

step down and was **INSTANTLY**

SiCK on Holly's shoulder, and that's only

because Holly has good reflexes—he was

almost sick on her head!

Finally, we all made it to the bottom and

started looking around with our torches.

Holly took a few steps, lighting up the

ground near some trickling water.

"Hey, look at this!" she said.

Holly pointed down and we gathered around her to see what she was looking at. There was a series of different **ANiMAL PRiNTS** on the ground, and they all seemed to be heading in the **SAMe DiRECTiON.**

Then I noticed something else. "Look, the tracks are heading **DOWNSTREAM!**"

Holly looked at me. "What is there

downstream?"

"The sewage treatment plant," I told her.

"**AH-HA!**" said Holly excitedly.

Then she frowned. "**HANG ON**

A MINUTE ... the sewage

treatment plant is downstream?

I thought you said this was an

AQUEDUCT!"

I looked at her. "It is ... sort of ... I

mean, it does conduct water—"

"–and sewage!" Danny chipped in

unhelpfully.

"–to the sewage treatment plant," I

finished.

Holly shuddered. "I think I'm going to be

sick," she said. **"I'M GETTING**

OUT OF HERE!"

Holly turned around and started

climbing up the first ladder she saw. She

STOPPED suddenly before she

got to the top.

Then she looked back down at us.

"Er ... does anyone know what that bleeping, **FLASHiNG** thing is doing up there on the ceiling?"

We crowded around Holly's ladder to have a closer look. Danny had seen something like it before.

"Well, I don't know a lot about explosives," he said, "but my dad is always blowing things up, and that looks **eXACTLY** like the sort of thing that could **BLOW SOMETHING UP**."

It took about a second for the information to register. Then we all panicked.

"EVERYBODY OUT OF HERE NOW!" I yelled. "I've just realized what's going on!"

We found the nearest manhole and climbed out of the sewer so fast that Percy didn't even have time to be sick on anyone.

We ran as fast as we could. When we thought we'd got to a safe distance, we hid.

I turned to Holly. "Holly, have you got your phone on you?"

"Yes," she replied.

"Then call the police straight away and tell them that there's about to be **A ROBBERY**."

Holly looked at me confused. "A robbery? Where?"

"In the jewelry shop," I told her.

Dad was right. It had been under my

nose all along!

We stayed **HIDDEN** until the

police arrived and closed off the

area. They quickly got to work and

DIFFUSED THE BOMB.

Then they came over to us with all of their

awkward questions.

The first awkward question was:

So, who would like to explain what you four are doing roaming around the sewers at half past four in the morning, dressed in garbage bags and vomit?

I thought I'd best handle this one. "We had an anonymous tip from someone who said that our **MISSING PETS** were down there."

PC McApple looked at me

SUSPICIOUSLY. "An

anonymous tip from whom?" he asked. He

had clearly just been dragged out of bed and his brain wasn't fully engaged yet.

"They didn't say," I told him patiently.

Then PC McApple received a call on his walkie talkie.

"This is PC Flatpack. We have apprehended four suspects fleeing from the crime scene in a white van. Over."

"Take them back to the station for questioning," PC McApple said. "I'll be right in. I just have to drop these kids off at their homes. Over."

He turned to us. "Now kids, let's get you home. You still haven't told me why you're dressed like that though."

Holly rolled her eyes at PC McApple. "Some people know nothing about fashion!"

We got PC McApple to drop us all off at my house. There, he called everyone else's parents who agreed to pick up their kids. It didn't take a **GENIUS** to work out that we were all going to be in **A LOT OF TROUBLE**.

Fortunately for me, Dad had had to go on a mission, or 'leave for London' as he put it, and Mom wouldn't be back from her trip yet, so Granny Meera was spending the night. She was quick to

make sure I was okay, tell

me off, and then rush into

the kitchen to make us

all a nice **CUP OF**

CARDAMOM COCOA

with spicy ginger cookies.

I peeled a note off the fridge that Dad

had left for me earlier. Then I went to

join Holly, Percy, and Danny as we all sat

around the table with our cocoa. Granny

Meera went upstairs to change out of her

pajamas into something more appropriate

for receiving a mob of angry parents at

the crack of dawn. We knew we didn't

have long to talk.

Holly turned to me. She wasn't happy.

"So ... **NO HARRIET THE**

HAMSTER. No pets at all, in fact.

Can you explain what just happened?"

"Yes, I think I can," I said. "It was the

JEWELRY SHOP ALL

ALONG."

"What do you mean, 'all along'?" Danny asked.

"I mean that nobody ever intended to break into the pet shop … that was an accident," I explained. "The robbers obviously got disoriented the first time that they went into the sewer, and ended up **BLOWiNG UP THE PET SHOP**. That's why they had to wait a few days before trying again. They needed to make sure the police weren't on to them."

Holly still looked puzzled. "Okay," she said, "but if they weren't interested in the pets, why did they bother taking them?"

I had to think about it for a little bit, then it seemed obvious. "Well, I suppose they wanted to **COVER UP THE REAL CRIME**. If they had just blown a hole

in the floor of the pet shop but hadn't

stolen anything, it would seem weird.

This way everybody thought they'd got

what they wanted, and **NOBODY**

SUSPECTED that they'd try to

rob the jewelry shop **AGAIN** a few

days later."

"Genius!" said Danny.

Percy nodded as he crunched his way

through the cookies Granny Meera had

put out for us.

"Okay," said Holly, "but this still doesn't tell us **WHAT HAPPENED TO ALL THE PETS**."

I nodded. "I know, but this does."

I took out the note that Dad had left me on the fridge, and placed it on the table. The note read:

Hope Farm—Animal Sanctuary

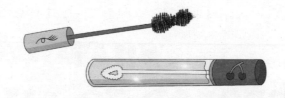

LOG ENTRY #8

Location: My bedroom

Status: Final report

It took quite a lot of convincing for

everyone's parents to allow us to visit

HOPE FARM ANIMAL

SANCTUARY on Saturday

morning. We'd all been told that we'd be doing **CHORES UNTIL WE GRADUATED**. I felt especially sorry for Danny and Percy. In their case, that might be a very long time.

Holly wasn't really allowed to visit the sanctuary. She and her mom were just going to stop by to pick up Harriet before going to Face Gunk to join the animal welfare group that was protesting outside the factory.

Apparently, when Holly had got home she'd noticed the corner of a little note sticking out from under Harriet the hamster's cage. It read:

I can't take it anymore! I'm running away to a place where I won't be treated like a toy.
Love, Harriet

Holly knew immediately that the note wasn't in Harriet's handwriting. This meant that her mom must have been in on it all along. When Holly confronted her mom, she came clean and told her that she and Harriet had **FAKED THE ESCAPE** so that Holly would learn to appreciate Harriet more. Holly's mom had left Harriet safely in Hope Farm's pet sanctuary to get some rest, but she had expected Holly to find the note straight away. As it turned out, taping the escape note to the bottom of the cage had not been her best idea.

Our parents stayed in their cars as Percy, Danny and I rang the doorbell and waited to be let in. It was a chilly morning and we could see our breath in the air. Holly and her mom joined us as we waited on the step. You could tell from the atmosphere that they had been arguing in the car, and that they would probably continue **ARGUING** as soon as they got the chance.

A very friendly looking lady greeted us as she opened the door.

"Good morning," she smiled, "I'm Janet Marble. I'm the owner of Hope Farm."

"Good morning," I replied. "I'm Mina, we spoke on the phone. My friends and I are **MISSING SOME PETS** and we wondered if they might have turned up here?"

"Well, they just might have done," said Miss Marble. "A lot of animals turned up suddenly last Monday."

Danny perked up. "Really? Last Monday? Do you think that the **ANIMALS THAT DISAPPEARED** from the pet shop might have turned up here?"

"I don't think so," I told him. "I know so."

I pulled out a piece of paper from my pocket and handed it to Miss Marble to look at.

"What is that?" Holly asked.

"Yesterday I found the telephone

number for the **PET SHOP** and

called the owner. I asked him to give me a list with descriptions of all the missing animals," I said.

We watched Miss Marble's surprised face as she read down the list.

Finally, she said, "**AMAZiNG**. **THEY'RE ALL HERE!** They started turning up last week. I thought that people were **ABANDONiNG** them outside, so I took them all in."

Percy turned to me. "Brilliant! But how did you know?"

"It was all thanks to Holly," I said. "She found all the **ANIMAL TRACKS IN THE SEWERS** heading downstream toward the sewage treatment plant. I knew that there was nothing else in this part of town apart from the **FACE GUNK FACTORY**

AND THIS ANIMAL SANCTUARY. I figured that

if I were a lost pet and I had to choose

between an animal sanctuary, a sewage

treatment plant, and a makeup factory, I

know where I'd go."

Holly's mom just had to say something.

  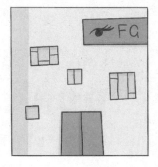

"Well, I think the animals are very lucky to have ended up here. Just imagine if they'd ended up next door at the Face Gunk factory! They'd all be **CAGED UP** in a laboratory now, having all those *horrible* products tested on them."

Holly rolled her eyes. "Mom! You really don't have a clue, do you? I already *told* you that Face Gunk **DON'T TEST THEIR PRODUCTS ON**

ANiMALS, but you won't listen

to me! I don't want to go to your stupid

protest! I know that those annoying

friends of yours have been intimidating

people and sending them **NASTY**

NOTeS. Even if it's for a good

cause, that's **NOT** okay, Mom. Look

at this one I found in the factory the

other day!"

Holly put her hand in her pocket and

produced a printed note that read:

STOP ANIMAL CRUELTY. KEEPING ANIMALS IN CAGES IS WRONG. RELEASE THE ANIMALS OR PAY THE PRICE.

I was shocked. I'd seen these words

before—they were the **exACT**

WORDS that the pet shop owner had

read out to PC McApple! They had been

on the note someone had pushed under

the pet shop door before the break-in.

'STOP ANIMAL CRUELTY.
KEEPING ANIMALS IN CAGES IS WRONG.
RELEASE THE ANIMALS OR PAY THE PRICE.'

It was important not to leap to any conclusions. "Okay," I said slowly, "but you found that note in the factory. What makes you think that your mom had anything to do with it?"

Holly pulled out another piece of paper from her pocket. She showed us the note Harriet had supposedly written to explain why she was running away. Then Holly turned over the piece of paper. It had been written on the back of a note with

the **EXACT SAME** words on it

as the other two.

STOP ANIMAL
CRUELTY.
KEEPING
ANIMALS IN
CAGES IS
WRONG.
RELEASE THE
ANIMALS OR PAY
THE PRICE.

Holly's mom looked very uncomfortable. "Look," she said. "I didn't print out the notes. **SOMEONE FROM THE ANIMAL RIGHTS GROUP DID.** There were a lot of them on the table at the last meeting. I must have picked up a handful and put them in my bag ... you know ... to use as note paper ..."

Holly's mom trailed off mid-sentence and turned to Holly.

"You were at the Face Gunk factory? You just said you found that note the other day at the Face Gunk factory. What on earth were you doing there, young lady?"

Holly looked really smug. "Oh ... didn't I tell you? I've been working there."

Holly's mom did not look impressed. "Working for that **GHASTLY PLACE?** Doing what?"

"Testing their makeup," said Holly.

Everybody's jaws dropped as Holly explained, "Actually Mom, you gave me the idea when you were going on about animals being **FORCED** to have makeup tested on them. I mean, that's really not fair … **I WANTED TO DO THAT!** So I popped in to speak to management, and started working there as an HTS—you know, a Human Test Subject."

Holly's mom did not look happy.

"Oh, you're in even **MORE TROUBLE** now, young lady! And what were they thinking, giving you work without asking for my permission first? How old did you tell them you were?! I can't believe you'd go behind

my back and work for that **AWFUL**

FACTORY–"

"I don't get it Mom," Holly interrupted.

"You should be happy! You don't want

the products to be tested on animals,

do you? And don't you always say that it

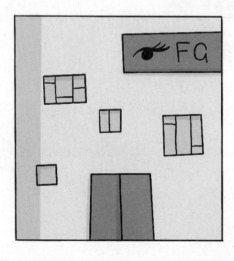

should be the people who use makeup that test it? Well, that's me: I use Face Gunk all the time, and **NOW I TEST FACE GUNK**.

What's your problem? This is my way of doing something nice for all the cute little animals, whilst getting a **FREE THREE-YEAR SUPPLY OF LIP GLOSS**."

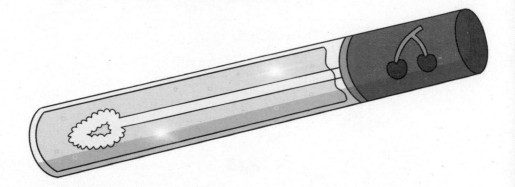

Holly's mom looked like she knew that something was wrong, but she couldn't quite put her finger on what.

Miss Marble decided to change the subject. "Anyway, you probably want **HARRIET THE HAMSTER** back," she said. "Your mom brought her to us to look after for a bit, but I think she's ready to go home."

Miss Marble handed Harriet back to Holly. Holly looked absolutely

DELIGHTED, although I kind of

got the feeling that Harriet looked a little

SAD to be back with Holly.

"Oh, **THANK YOU!**" Holly gushed. "I'll take great care of her! Come on Harriet, we're going to get matching tiaras."

At that, Holly turned on her heel, waving goodbye to everyone as she walked away. Her mom followed, still looking confused. I watched Harriet the hamster as Holly carried her away. I could have sworn I heard her little hamster voice saying, *"Help me, please help me!"*, but it was probably just my imagination. **PROBABLY**.

221

Miss Marble turned to me. "Anyway, if that's everything, I'd love to have the pet shop's phone number. I'm sure that the owner would like to know where all the missing animals are. And if you know anyone who would like to **ADOPT A PET**, we have plenty here that need good homes."

I thought about it. Maybe I should ask Mom and Dad if I could adopt a pet. After all, I'd **NEVER** had a pet before, and as a result I was about to

get a **TERRIBLE GRADE**

on my project 'Slugly Bugly the

Predatory Slug and the Final Hours

of Sammy the Earthworm'. **THEN**

I REMEMBERED

SOMETHING.

"Oh! I have one more question: have

you found a pet toad? Or a box of snails?"

Danny looked at Miss Marble hopefully ...

but it wasn't to be.

She shook her head. "I'm very sorry, but I'm afraid I haven't seen any **TOADS** or **SNAiLS**."

Danny looked gutted.

"But I'll be sure to call you if they turn up," she added quickly. We said our goodbyes.

Danny, Percy and I stopped in the car park. Danny's eyes were welling up. I knew that our work at the sanctuary was over, but I couldn't leave him until we had worked out what had happened to **SUPERDOG**.

"Okay, let's go over the information one more time," I told him. "You last saw **SUPERDOG** on the afternoon of the presentation, when he was in a brown shoebox. After you finished the presentation, what did you do with the shoebox?'

Danny sniffed. "I put it in my black bag."

"Can anyone remember what Herbie Fisher did with his **SNAiLS** when he finished his presentation?" I asked.

Danny shook his head.

"I think he said that he put the box in his bag. It was black too," Percy volunteered, "but then, when he got home the snails weren't there."

"Danny," I said. "Can you remember what you did with your bag when you got home?"

Danny thought about it. "I left it in ... no, wait ... I took it upstairs ..."

Danny clearly wasn't sure. I needed to jog his memory. "Okay, let's break it down. How did you get home from school? Did you take the bus?"

Suddenly, Danny's eyes **WIDENED**. "The last time I saw my black bag was when I threw it in the boot of Mom's car when she picked me up from school!"

Danny ran toward his mom's car and

opened the boot. There in the back was

a **CRUMPLED**

BLACK BAG.

Danny stopped in his

tracks. "I can't open it. What

if Superdog is …?"

"Don't say it!" said Percy,

putting his hands over his ears.

I took the black bag and unzipped

it. There were two brown shoeboxes

inside. One of them was empty. The other contained a **VERY FAT TOAD** and a lot of **EMPTY SNAIL SHELLS**.

Superdog looked at Danny and belched, whilst Percy **THREW UP** in the background.

All the **MYSTERIES** had finally been cleared up!

"Well," I said. "It looks like Herbie Fisher accidentally put his snail farm in your rucksack with Superdog—**LUCKY FOR SUPERDOG!** So, I guess we'd better go back to the animal sanctuary. I think you owe Herbie a new pet."

Danny, Percy and I turned back toward Hope Farm.

"What sort of pet do you think makes a good replacement for a box of snails?" Danny asked.

"I don't know," I replied. "Maybe you should go for something that won't get eaten this time—like a hedgehog!"

We parted ways and each went home to get on with our chores.

NEW SHOP
OPENING SOON:
GREENVILLE PET SUPPLIES

The pet shop **STAYED CLOSED** over the next few weeks while they had their floor repaired. After that, they reopened as a pet food shop.

NEW SHOP
OPENING SOON:
GREENVILLE PET SUPPLIES

The pet shop owner had spoken to Miss Marble, and she decided that the sanctuary was a better place for the animals to live until they **FOUND PROPER HOMES**.

Harriet the hamster now has more than

100,000 FOLLOWERS

on social media, and Holly has become

her stylist and manager. I don't know what

Danny and Percy are up to. Maybe I'll find

out at school next week—it's sure to be

SOMETHiNG GROSS.

Now that I'm fully caught up on my

NOTeS, I'd better wrap this up.

I've got a lot to do for school—I have to

come up with a project for Chocolate

Handstand Construction Week.

This is **MiNA MiSTRY** signing

off on another solved case.

THE
CASE OF THE
DISAPPEARING
PETS

DEC 2021

LOOK OUT FOR THE NEXT INVESTIGATION

MINA MISTRY

(SORT OF) INVESTIGATES

THE CASE OF THE BICYCLE THIEF

Sweet Cherry